Based on the television series *The Wubbulous World of Dr. Seuss*™,
produced by Jim Henson Productions, Inc.

Library of Congress Cataloging-in-Publication Data
Rabe, Tish. Who are you, Sue Snue? /
by Tish Rabe ; adapted from a script by Will Ryan. p. cm.
"Based on the television series The wubbulous world of Dr. Seuss."
SUMMARY: Of all the things that Sue Snue might decide to do
she wants to be herself and do what she wants to do.
ISBN 0-679-88636-2 (trade). — ISBN 0-679-98636-7 (lib.bdg.)
[1. Individuality—Fiction. 2. Stories in rhyme.] I. Ryan, Will.
II. The wubbulous world of Dr. Seuss (Television program). III. Title.
PZ8.3.R1145Wh 1997 [E]—dc21 96-49448

Printed in the United States of America 10 9 8 7 6 5 4 3 2 1

The Wubbulous world of Dr. Seuss™

Who Are You, Sue Snue?

by TISH RABE

adapted from a script
by WILL RYAN

illustrated by
TOM BRANNON

Random House / Jim Henson Productions

Happy birthday to you!
Happy birthday to you!
Yes, you, Sue Snue.
Happy birthday to you—

Ms. Susan Bocks
Dutter Docks
Berklummer Snue!

Now, Sue, that you
are older than two,
it's time for you
to choose something to do.

Will you, like Uncle Bocks,
make left-footed red socks?

Will you, like Uncle Docks,
make right-footed green socks?

Red socks?
Green socks?
Yellow or blue?
Susan Bocks
Dutter Docks,
what will you do?

Or like Uncle Dutter,
will you be a cake-cutter?
Uncle Dutter cuts cake, Sue.
Is that good for you, too—

Ms. Susan Bocks
Dutter Docks
Berklummer Snue?

Or will you be a zummer
like your Uncle Berklummer?

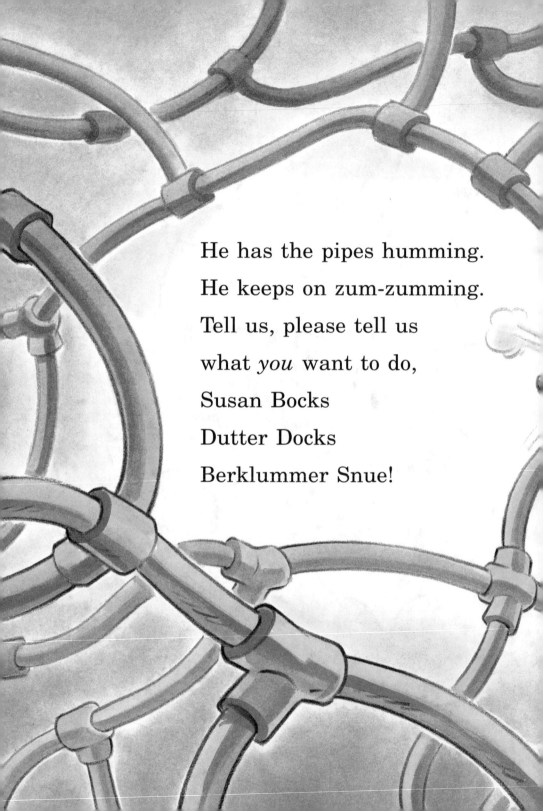

He has the pipes humming.
He keeps on zum-zumming.
Tell us, please tell us
what *you* want to do,
Susan Bocks
Dutter Docks
Berklummer Snue!

Or will you, dear Sue,
do something all new?
Will you be
a cowpoke...
and poke lots of cows?

Will you be
a singer...
and take lots of bows?

Will you be a butcher?

Will you be a baker?

Or will you, Sue Snue,

be an ice-cream-cone maker?

Ms. Susan Bocks
Dutter Docks
Berklummer Snue,
tell us: What is it
that you want to do?

Will you be a farmer
and grow things to eat?

Will you be a foot doctor
and doctor our feet?

Will you be an astronaut...

...soaring through space?

Will you be a runner
running a race?

Will you be a teacher?
Yes! Be one of those!

Or maybe a tailor
and tailor our clothes?

Will you be president?
Hail to the chief!

Or maybe a police officer who catches a thief?

A bullfighter?

A skywriter?

A canner of peas?

A trainer of fleas?

Tell us, oh, tell us,
yes, tell us, Sue, please!
Tell us, Sue Snue,
just *what* you want to do,
Susan Bocks
Dutter Docks
Berklummer Snue!

"STOP, EVERYBODY!
I know what I'll do.
I'll just be myself,
my whole self
and not you.
I'll be true to myself.
That's *just* what I'll do!
No uncle or aunt
can tell me 'You can't!'
No mother or pop
can tell me 'Please stop!'
I'll do what *I* want to.
That's what I'll do!"

Ms. Susan Bocks
Dutter Docks
Berklummer Snue—
good for you!